This book has been donated to
The Concord Library in the honor of

Tim Fowler

this 31st day of July, 2017 _[signature]_
President

ROTARY
SERVING
HUMANITY

Rotary
Club of Concord

From **WOLF** to *WOOF!*

The Story of Dogs

...and those who love them

HUDSON TALBOTT

Nancy Paulsen Books

NANCY PAULSEN BOOKS
an imprint of Penguin Random House LLC
375 Hudson Street
New York, NY 10014

Nancy Paulsen Books is a registered trademark of Penguin Random House LLC.
Library of Congress Cataloging-in-Publication Data
Talbott, Hudson.   From wolf to woof : the story of dogs / Hudson Talbott.   pages cm
Summary: Beginning with two orphans, a prehistoric boy and a wolf cub, imagines how the bond
between man and wolf might have formed and looks at how it changed through their shared
history as wolves became domesticated and diversified into more than 400 breeds of dog.
Includes bibliographical references.
[1. Human-animal relationships—Fiction. 2. Dogs—Fiction. 3. Wolves—Fiction.
4. Prehistoric peoples—Fiction.] I. Title.   PZ7.T153Fro 2016   [E]—dc23   2015016978
Manufactured in China by RR Donnelly Asia Printing Solutions Ltd.
ISBN 978-0-399-25404-8
1 3 5 7 9 10 8 6 4 2

Text set in Clavo. The art was done in watercolors,
colored pencil, and ink on Arches watercolor paper.

For Jay

I love telling
this story

Long, long ago . . .
before humans and dogs were friends . . .
in fact, long before there *were* dogs,
                              there were . . .

. . . wolves!

Wolves roamed the earth freely, in packs.
A wolf pack is a family group that works as a team to hunt and care for their young. The leader eats first, followed by the lower-ranking wolves. Without a pack, a wolf could starve to death.

There was once an orphaned wolf pup who tagged along behind a pack, hoping to be accepted. But the leader kept chasing him away.

The pup decided to
show the pack that
they needed him.

I'll stand guard and
warn them of enemies!

The "enemies" were humans, who
hunted wolves for fur and for food.
The pup kept a sharp lookout all day.

But then darkness fell.

I'm a wolf
I'm a wolf
I'm a big bad

WOOOOO

It was the enemy!
The pup had never seen
a little one before.

OHOOOHUMAN!

Shhh! Quiet, wolf!
I'll throw you this bone
if you stop howling!

The boy was an orphan, too, trying
to feed himself from the scraps that
humans had left behind.
He tossed a bone to the pup.

The pup grabbed the bone
and dashed into the night.

He couldn't believe his luck!

He chewed on it for days until there
was nothing left but a delicious memory.

But soon, hunger drove him back to the scrap heap.

Another bone was tossed his way, and again, the pup dashed away with it.

Then one day, the pup did something that
wasn't very wolf-like.
   He wandered back, edged nearer to the boy,
and dropped the bone.

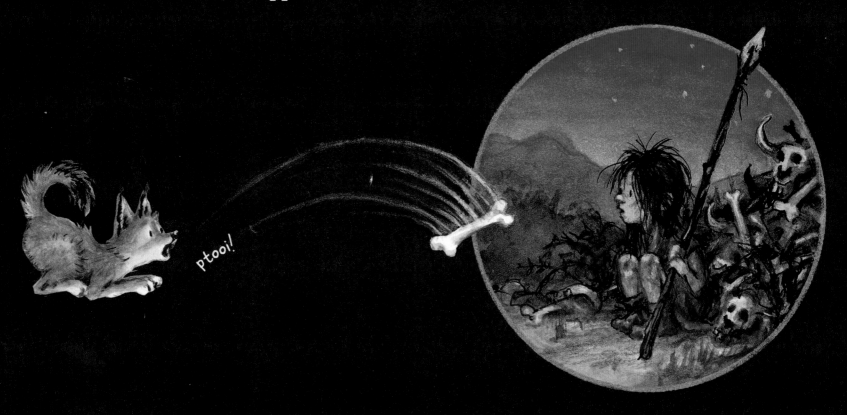

ptooi!

The boy picked up the bone and tossed it back.
   Again, the wolf pup caught it and dropped it
nearer the boy.
   Over and over, the boy threw it back, each time
moving a little closer.

Soon they were close enough to touch.

And that's when
everything changed.

They became a great team, hunting and playing
together, and keeping each other warm at night.

Before long, others found their way to the boy's fire.
They were all misfits—low-ranking wolves and
children who wandered in search of food, with no friends
or family of their own. But now they had each other.

Over the years, the little tribe of outcasts
grew bigger and bigger.
They still had their run-ins . . .

sometimes with wolves . . .

sometimes with other humans.

But one thing was plain to see . . .

they ate better than anyone!

The secret was in the teamwork.
Wolves surrounded the prey
so hunters could spear it from
a distance.

How do we get our own wolves?

Everyone worked together
and shared the food.
No one was left out.

The little tribe of friends went on
hunting together for the rest of their lives.
The wolves knew that their best chance
of survival was to stay with the humans.
They were a little less wild but a lot more safe.

Most other wolves stayed far
away, remaining wild and free.
But for those who dared to
try their luck with the humans,
a very different future lay ahead.

Over thousands of years, the wolves' sizes and shapes
changed to suit their lives with the humans. Things were
changing for the humans, too. They no longer had to roam
far and wide in search of food.

With the help of the wolves, the humans could stay in one place
and call it home, keeping their own herds nearby. That gave them time
to plant seeds and harvest crops. They had been hunters and gatherers.
Now they were becoming herders and farmers.

And the wolves were becoming . . .

. . .dogs!

As humans changed, dogs changed with them.
When humans had needs, dogs were there to help.

Guarding

Hunting

Herding

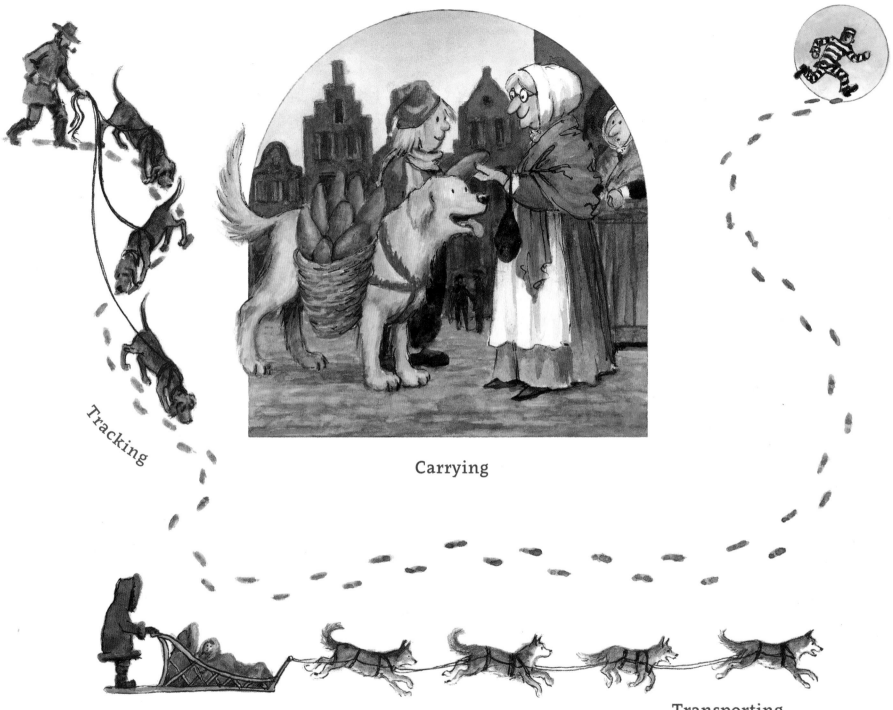

Tracking

Carrying

Transporting

Searching

Rescuing

Guiding

Comforting

So that brings us to where we are today . . .

. . . and of course—
the all-important
bed warming.

Dogs come in more shapes and sizes than any other animal—over 400 breeds and countless mixes.

The wolves are still out there, but it's getting
harder for them to live wild and free anymore.
They need our help if they are to survive.

Lucky for all of us that a few of them chose to join up with humans long ago. That's how dogs became dogs! And humans became, well, a little more human. They all took a chance on friendship and it paid off. You might even call it . . .

a howling success!

Author's Note

In every world culture, there is a traditional tale called a "myth of origin," a story that answers one of life's basic questions: *Where did we come from?* I've always been curious about the deep friendship we have with dogs and thought a dog's myth of origin would be fun to pursue. But in doing the research for this book, I discovered just how deeply intertwined their story is with our own. While it is true that dogs evolved from wolves due to their contact with us, what fascinated me was how much we evolved due to our contact with them. Human civilization and dogs evolved together—over thousands of years, at different locations, with many false starts and infinite variations. How do you make a story out of all that? Daunted at first, I remembered that this is exactly why mythology exists. A myth reveals a greater truth about life in the form of a simple story. I loved Greek mythology growing up. Now it was my turn to spin one of my own. I hope that this story of the dog's origin illustrates not just how they became dogs, but how they became our best friends.

For more information about what you can do to help
save wolves and other endangered wildlife, please visit:
Defenders of Wildlife at www.defenders.org
Predator Defense at www.predatordefense.org
National Wildlife Federation at www.nwf.org

For Further Reading

Children's Books

Pfeffer, Wendy. *Wolf Pup.* New York: Sterling Children's Books, 2011.
Simon, Charnan. *Wolves.* New York: Scholastic, 2012.
Simon, Seymour. *Wolves.* New York: HarperCollins, 1993.

Adult Books

Derr, Mark. *How the Dog Became the Dog.* New York: Overlook Press, 2011.
Kluger, Jeffrey, ed. "The Animal Mind." Special issue, *Time*, August 2014.
Miklósi, Ádám. *Dog Behaviour, Evolution, and Cognition.* New York: Oxford University Press, 2007.
Serpell, James, ed. *The Domestic Dog.* New York: Cambridge University Press, 1995.
Wang, Xiaoming, and Richard H. Tedford. *Dogs: Their Fossil Relatives and Evolutionary History.*
New York: Columbia University Press, 2008.